Food +
Farming

The Thief of Bracken Farm

First published in the UK in 2007 by
QED Publishing
A Quarto Group company
226 City Road
London EC1V 2TT
www.qed-publishing.co.uk

ISBN 978 1 84538 639 9

Written by Emma Barnes
Edited by Clare Weaver
Designed by Susi Martin
Illustrated by Hannah Wood
Consultancy by Anne Faundez

Publisher Steve Evans
Creative Director Zeta Davies
Senior Editor Hannah Ray

Printed and bound in China

The Thief
of
Bracken Farm

Emma Barnes

Illustrated by
Hannah Wood

QED Publishing

QED

Some very funny things were happening at Bracken Farm.

"Where is my hat?" asked Farmer Jones.

"It's on your head!" shouted Ted and Bess.

Farmer Jones was always losing his hat. And it was always on his head.

"No, it's not," said Farmer Jones.
It was true. The hat was not there.

"In the tractor!" shouted the children.

But the hat was not there.

"In the dairy!" they yelled.

But the hat was not there.

"We'll look for it," the children said. They went to the farmhouse. But they couldn't find the hat anywhere.

What's more, when they looked about, they saw that lots of others things had vanished, too.

Mrs Jones had lost her scarf. The baby had lost her mittens. The cat's blanket had gone from her basket. And Ted couldn't find his homework anywhere!

"Poor Marmalade!" said Bess.
"She'll be cold without her blanket."

"Never mind that," said Ted.
"I'll be in big trouble without my homework. I think there's a thief!"

"A thief?" said Bess.
"Why would a thief want your homework? I think there's a ghost!"

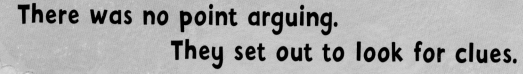

There was no point arguing.
They set out to look for clues.

First, they went to the orchard.
They saw lots of apples and pears,
but no sign of a thief.

Next, they went to the fields. They saw Adam the shepherd and Nell the sheepdog and fifty-four woolly sheep...

but no sign of a thief.

Then they went to the farmyard. They saw hens and ducks and Tansy the goat and...

There was somebody in Tansy's pen!
"I think the thief is stealing Tansy,"
Ted whispered.

The two children
crept closer. **And closer.**

They were standing right
next to the pen.

"STOP THIEF!"
they shouted.

The thief fell over. Only it wasn't a thief.
It was Miss Sanders the vet.
"You gave me a fright!" she said.

The children explained that they were
looking for the thief of Bracken Farm.

"I wasn't stealing Tansy," said Miss Sanders.
"I was bandaging her foot. Wait a minute!
What's happened to the bandage?"

"Maybe the thief took it," said Ted.

But the thief hadn't taken it. Tansy was eating it!

"Maybe Tansy ate the other things, too," said Bess. "Goats eat anything."

Miss Sanders didn't think so. She said that if Tansy had eaten a hat, a scarf, mittens, the cat's blanket and Ted's homework she would have a bad tummy, not a bad leg.

Just then, they heard a shout from the stables. They went to see what had happened.

"It's Marmalade!" said Mrs Jones. "It's time for her tea. I've looked everywhere. She's gone!"

"Oh no!" said Ted. "The thief took her!"

Everybody was very sad. Nobody cared any more about
Mr Jones's hat or Ted's homework or any of the other things.
But they all loved Marmalade the cat.

They were so sad that they were very,
very quiet. And because they were so
quiet, they heard a funny noise.

"Eehoooooooowww!"

"I told you there was
a ghost!" said Bess.

But Ted went over to the feed cupboard.
He opened the door...

And there was Marmalade! She had made herself a nest. She had used Farmer Jones's hat, the scarf, the mittens, her blanket and Ted's homework.

She had four new kittens, too!

Notes for Teachers and Parents

- The first time you read the book to the children, enjoy the story, the humour, the excitement of what will happen next and the rhythm of the words. Build up the suspense.

- Let the children try to guess who is the thief, and what else they might have taken. Then let the children take it in turns to try and read the story aloud, helping them with any difficult words. Remember to praise the children for their efforts in reading the book.

- Discussing the characters and story afterwards with children helps maintain interest and consolidate knowledge. Who is their favourite character? What is their favourite animal? Was it a big surprise that Marmalade was the thief? Or were there clues early on?

- Play the 'memory tray' game. On a tray, set out the objects that went missing in the story – a hat, mittens, a scarf, a blanket and some homework. Ask the children to study the tray for a minute. Then cover the tray with a cloth. How many objects can the children remember?

- The children can then make lists of the objects and learn to spell each word. Make a poster showing all the objects taken, with the word written alongside each picture.

- Encourage the children to create their own stories about a thieving animal. For example, magpies often take shiny objects. What would go missing on the farm if a magpie were the thief? What kind of things might a magpie take from the room the children are in? Or from a school playground?

- This story also lends itself to group artwork and collage work. Encourage the children to make separate drawings or paintings of the cat, each kitten and all of the missing objects. These can then be mounted together on a large piece of paper to make a picture of Marmalade and her kittens. Real wool, bits of shredded paper, etc can be glued onto the display to make a group collage.

- Help the children to make a wall display of the farm itself, with a tractor, farmhouse and all the different characters and animals. Incorporate lots of different materials – cotton-wool for the sheep, bits of foil on the tractor, felt, cloth, leaves and twigs, etc. Another approach is to cut out pictures of animals from magazines to be glued onto the display. Words can be stuck onto the picture, identifying the animals and the sounds they make, to encourage word-recognition.

- Dens and hiding-places appeal strongly to children's imaginations. Encourage them to imagine they have a secret hiding-place. Where would it be? In a cupboard or hollow tree? A cave? A forgotten attic? What would they keep there? What would they eat? Would they have a companion – a pet, a wild animal or a toy? Find words together to describe the den – spooky, cosy, dark, poky, secret, etc. Let them draw a picture of their den.